The Mermaid Dives In

By Sheila Sweeny Higginson
Based on the episode by Kent Redeker
Based on the series created by Chris Nee
Illustrated by Character Building Studio
and the Disney Storybook Artists

PRESS
New York

Finally, summer is here!
Doc McStuffins can't wait to play in the park with her friends.

2

Mom smooths sunscreen on Doc's skin.
Now she's ready for some fun in the sun!
"Is it okay if I take my toys and go play in the wading pool?" Doc asks.
"Sure," says Mom. "I'll keep an eye on you."

Doc wheels her wagon to the wading pool.
Her stethoscope begins to glow!
"Hi, guys!" Doc says as her friends come to life.

"I finally get to go swimming!" Stuffy cheers.
He jumps into the pool. Doc catches Stuffy in the nick of time.
"You and Lambie can't go in the water," Doc laughs.
"You're not water toys."

But there *is* a water toy at the other side of the pool.
She has long, flowing hair and a shimmering tail.
"It's a mermaid!" Lambie gasps. "They're like the princesses of the sea!"

Doc and Stuffy walk over to the other side of the pool.
Then Doc brings the mermaid to life with her magic stethoscope.
"Hello dilly scrumptious," the mermaid says. "My name is Melinda."

"I'd love to watch you swim," Lambie says shyly.

"Very well," Melinda says. "Prepare to be amazed!"

Doc takes a hoop out of the wagon and hands it to Surfer Girl.

"Take this to the center of the pool so Melinda can jump through it."

"Here I go!" Melinda calls. "It will be the most amazing water leap you've ever seen!"
Melinda splashes into the pool. But then she disappears!
"Hey, like, where'd she go?" asks Surfer Girl.

"I see her!" Bronty calls. "She's at the bottom of the pool!"
Doc reaches into the pool and rescues Melinda.
"Did you mean to do that?" Doc asks her.
"No," Melinda says. "I don't know why I sank to the bottom."

10

"I don't know, either," says Doc. "I'm worried something might be wrong with you."

"Wrong? I don't think so," says Melinda. "Mermaids are perfect."

"No one is perfect," Doc explains. "I think I should give you a checkup."

First, Doc checks Melinda's heart with her stethoscope.
"Your heartbeat sounds just as pretty as you are," says Doc.
Then she listens to Melinda's lungs.
"Your lungs sound good, too," Doc adds.

"Now I'm going to check your tail," Doc says. She asks Melinda to push with her tail.
Melinda tries, but she can't do it. "Is something wrong with me?" she asks.
Doc shrugs. "Has anyone ever wound up your winder-upper?"

"I didn't even know I had one!" Melinda says.

A-ha! Doc McStuffins has a diagnosis.

"You have a case of Stuck-Winder-Upperitis," she tells Melinda.

"Is that serious?" Melinda asks.

Doc shakes her head. "I can fix it right up!"
She works on Melinda's winder-upper until it's unstuck.
"Got it!" Doc says.
Then Lambie winds the winder and Melinda's tail starts to flap!

"My tail is flapping!" Melinda cheers.
"Get ready for a wonderful mermaid leaping show!"

Melinda splashes into the pool, but she sinks again!
"Oh, dear!" she cries. "I'm going down!"

Doc reaches into the pool and rescues Melinda again.
"Oh, Doc!" Melinda cries. "I'm a mermaid! I should be able to swim and leap and do all sorts of tricks. But I just keep sinking."

"Did you have this problem when you took swimming lessons?" Doc asks.

"What's that?" Melinda wonders.

"That's when someone teaches you how to swim. You took them, right?"

"No," Melinda says. "Do I need swimming lessons?"

"Everyone should take swimming lessons," Doc explains.
"I had so much fun learning to swim!"
Melinda is excited and wants to take swimming lessons, too!

"Let me handle this one," says Surfer Girl.
"I used to be a lifeguard, so I gave swimming lessons all the time!"

First, Surfer Girl shows Melinda how to stroke with her arms.
"That's it!" says Surfer Girl.
Then she shows Melinda how to kick with her tail.
"Great job," Surfer Girl says.

Soon Melinda starts to swim on her own.
"You're an amazing swimmer!" Lambie calls.
"I'm so glad I took swimming lessons," Melinda says. "I finally feel like
a real mermaid!"

This time, when Melinda the Mermaid leaps through the hoop, she swims like a real mermaid, too!